MW00425938

Playing

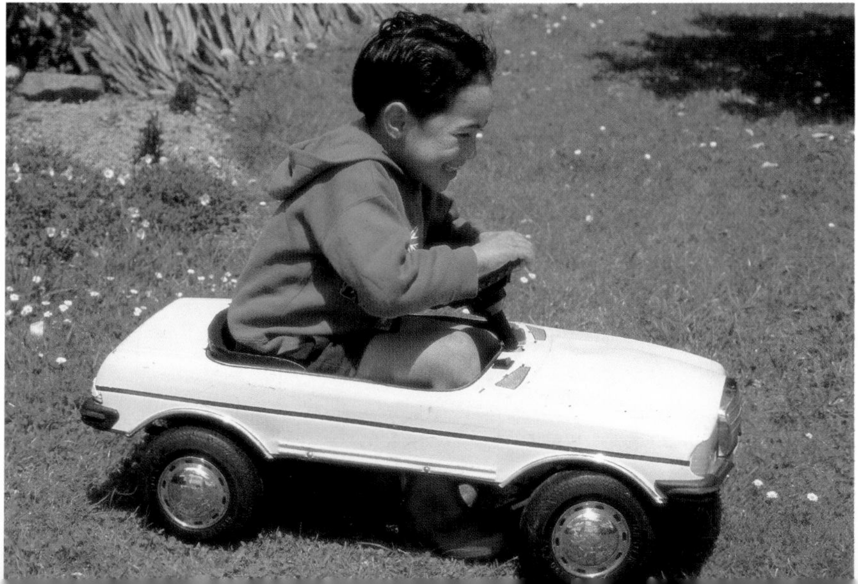

I am in the box.

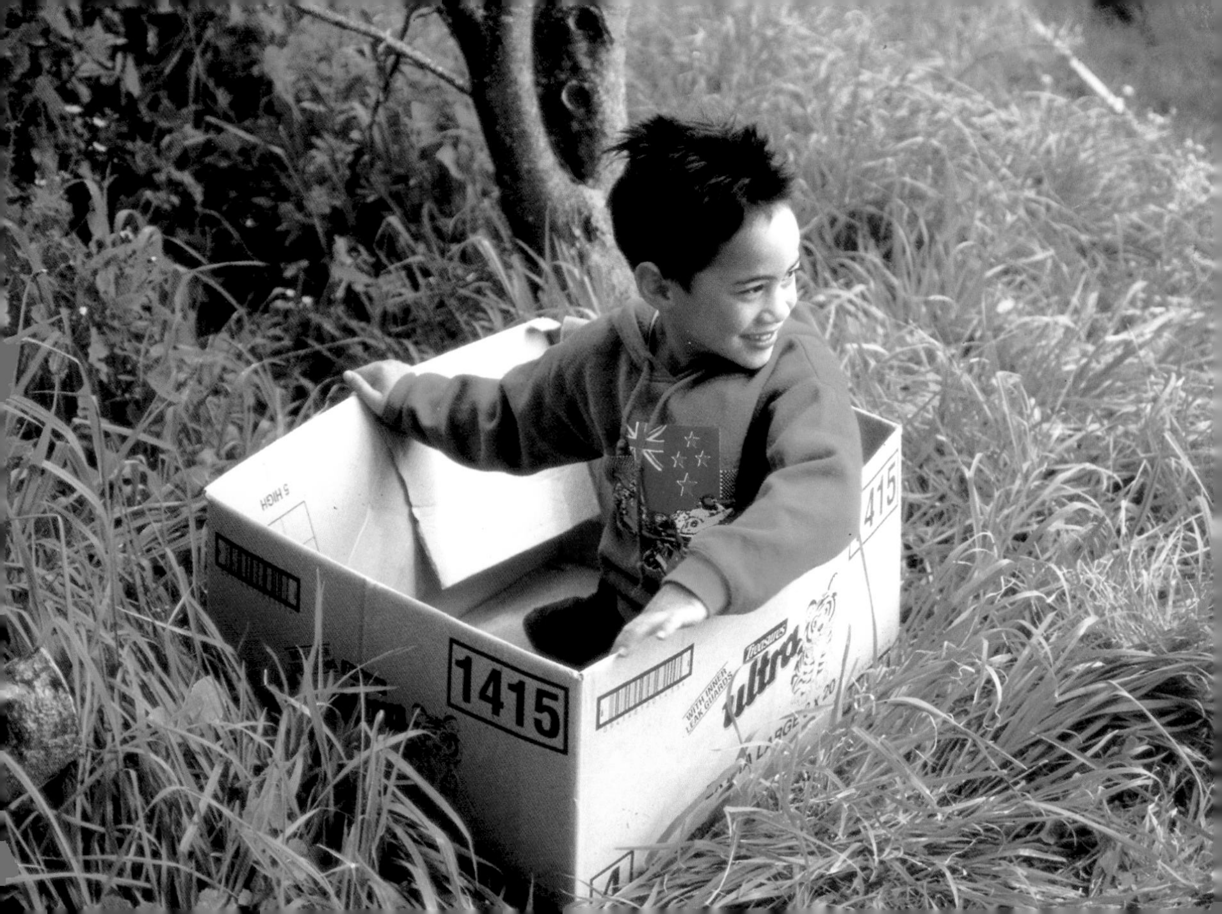
1415
415
WITH INNER
LEAK GUARDS
ultra

I am in the car.

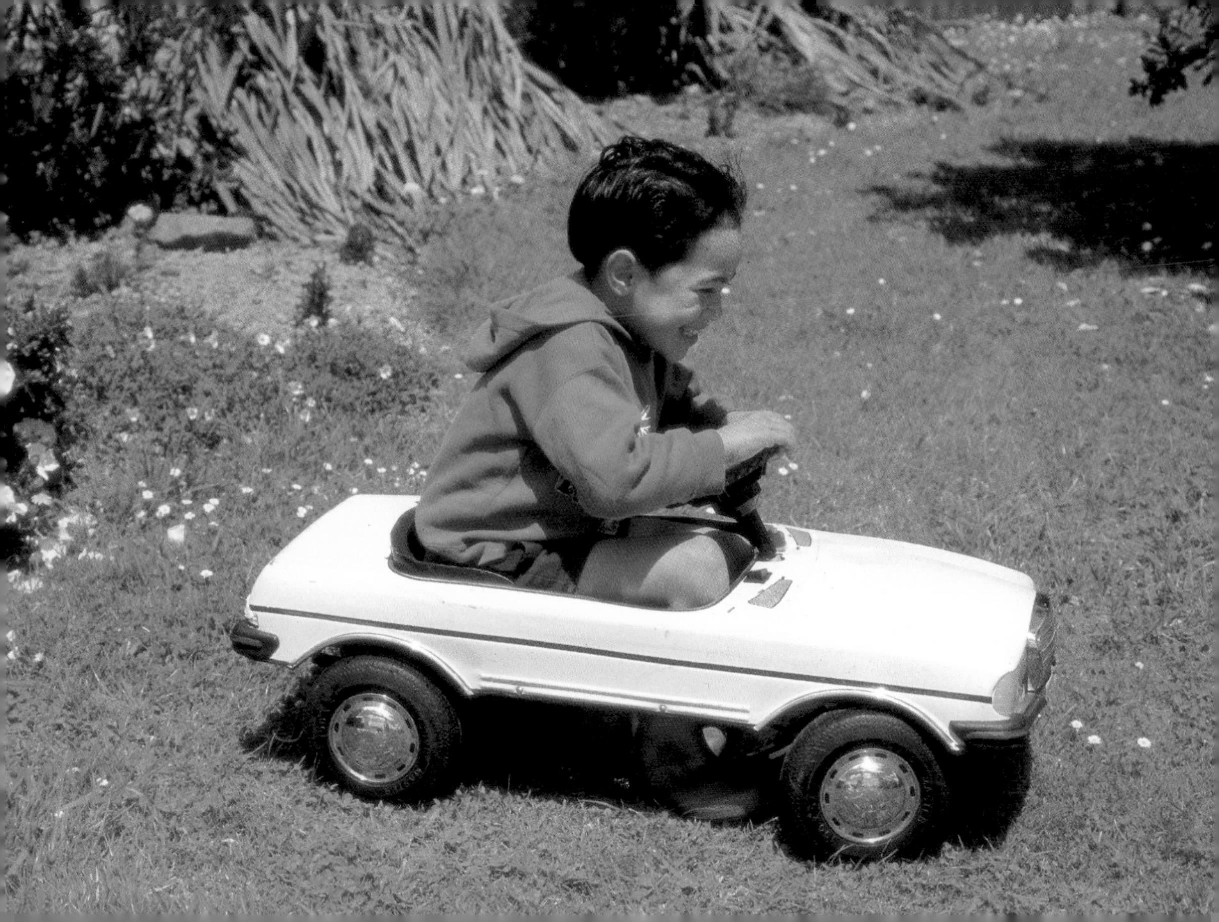

I am in the tent.

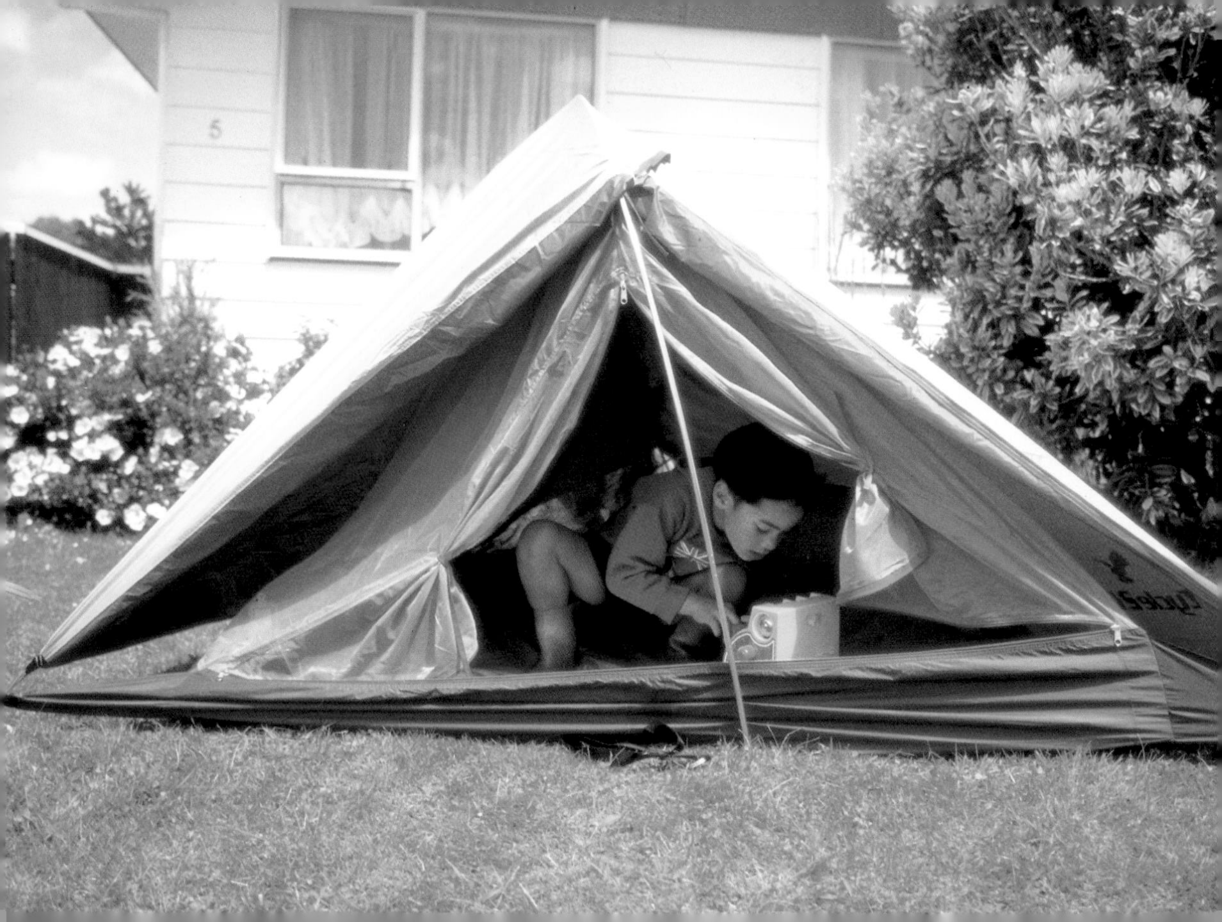
5

I am in the sandbox.

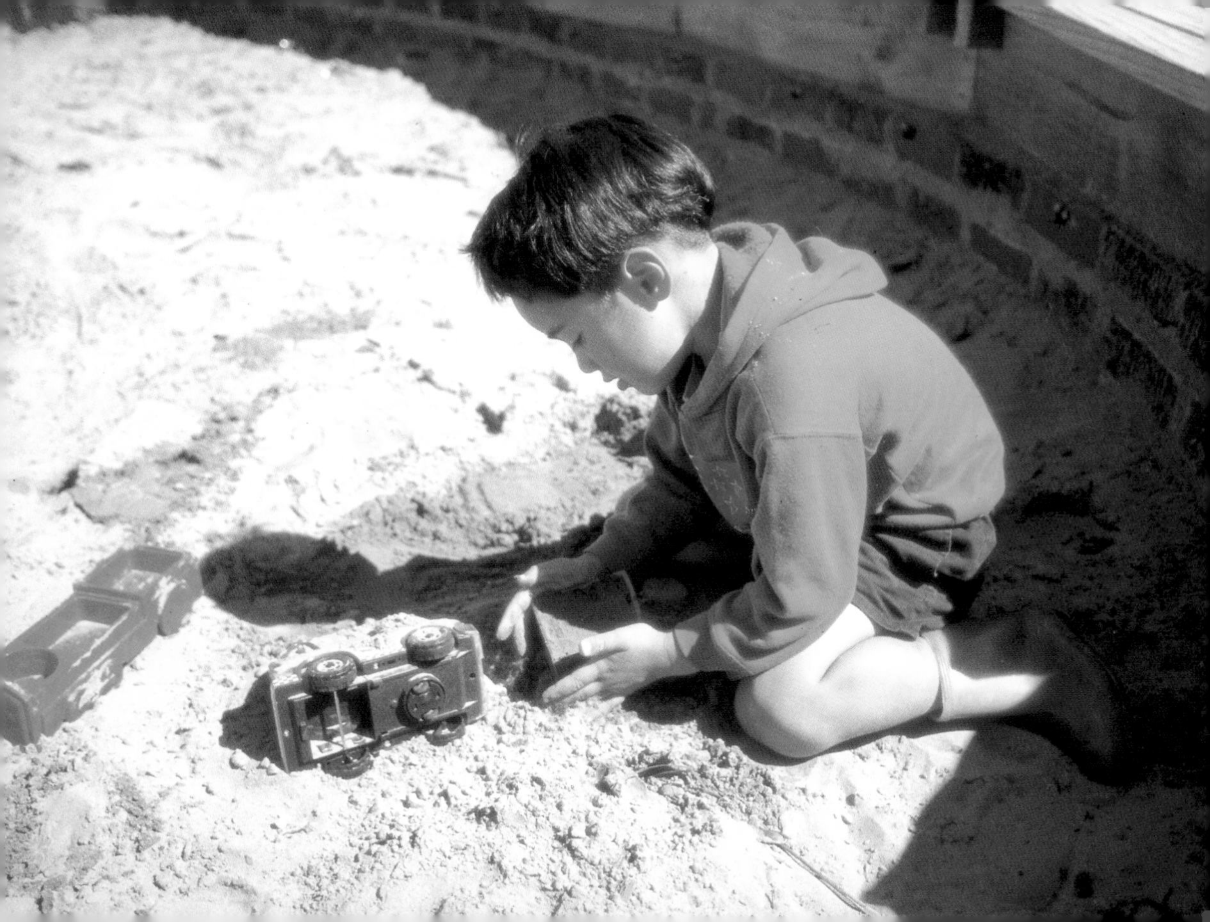

I am in the playhouse.

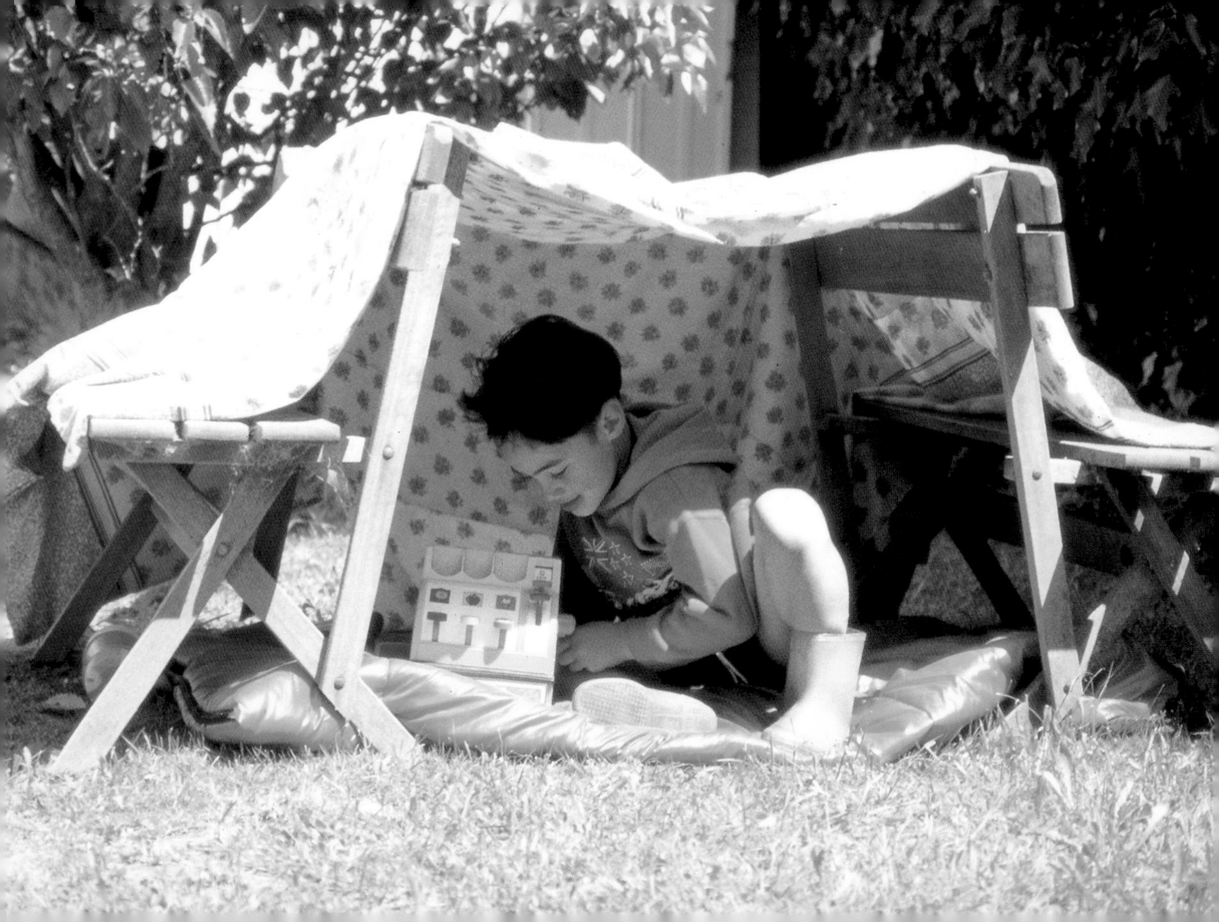

I am in the tree.

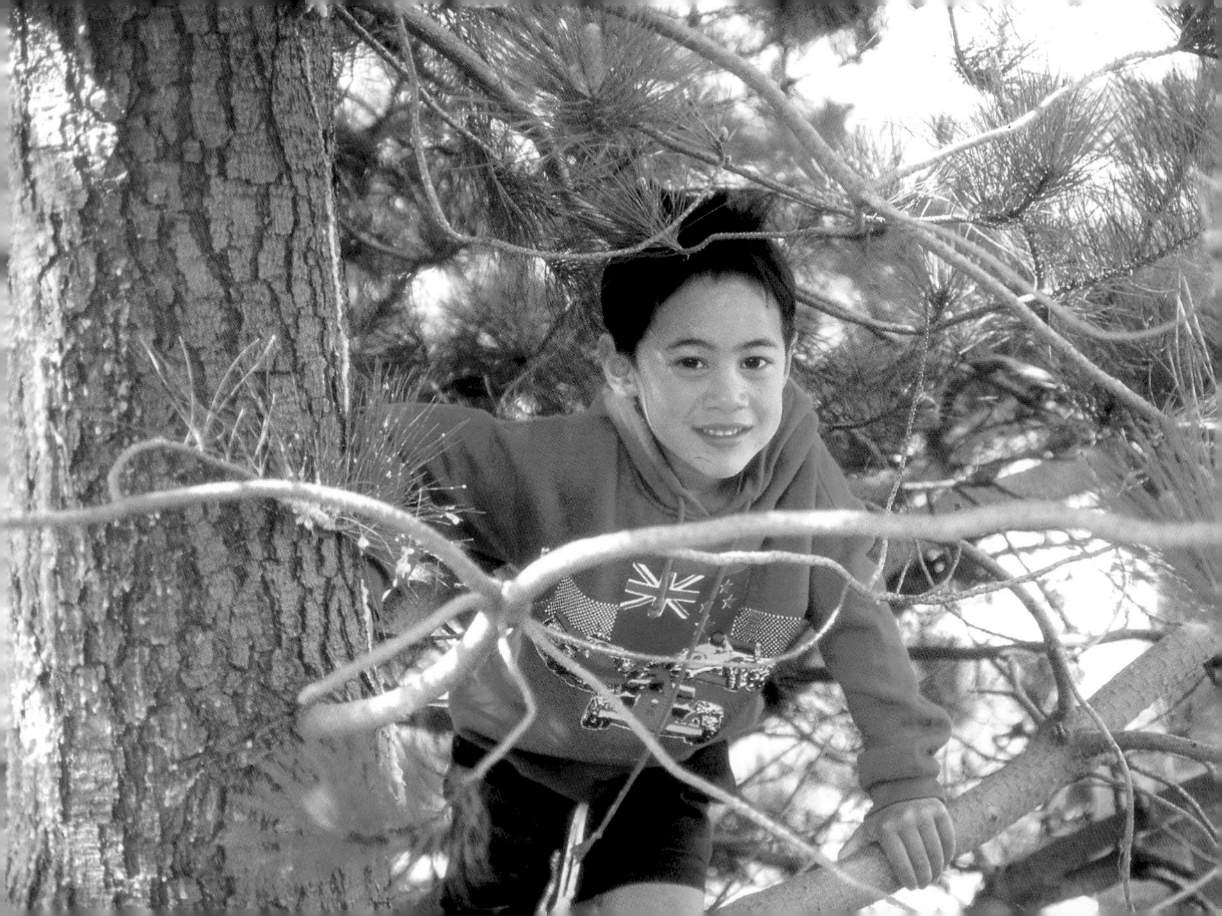

I am in the bathtub.

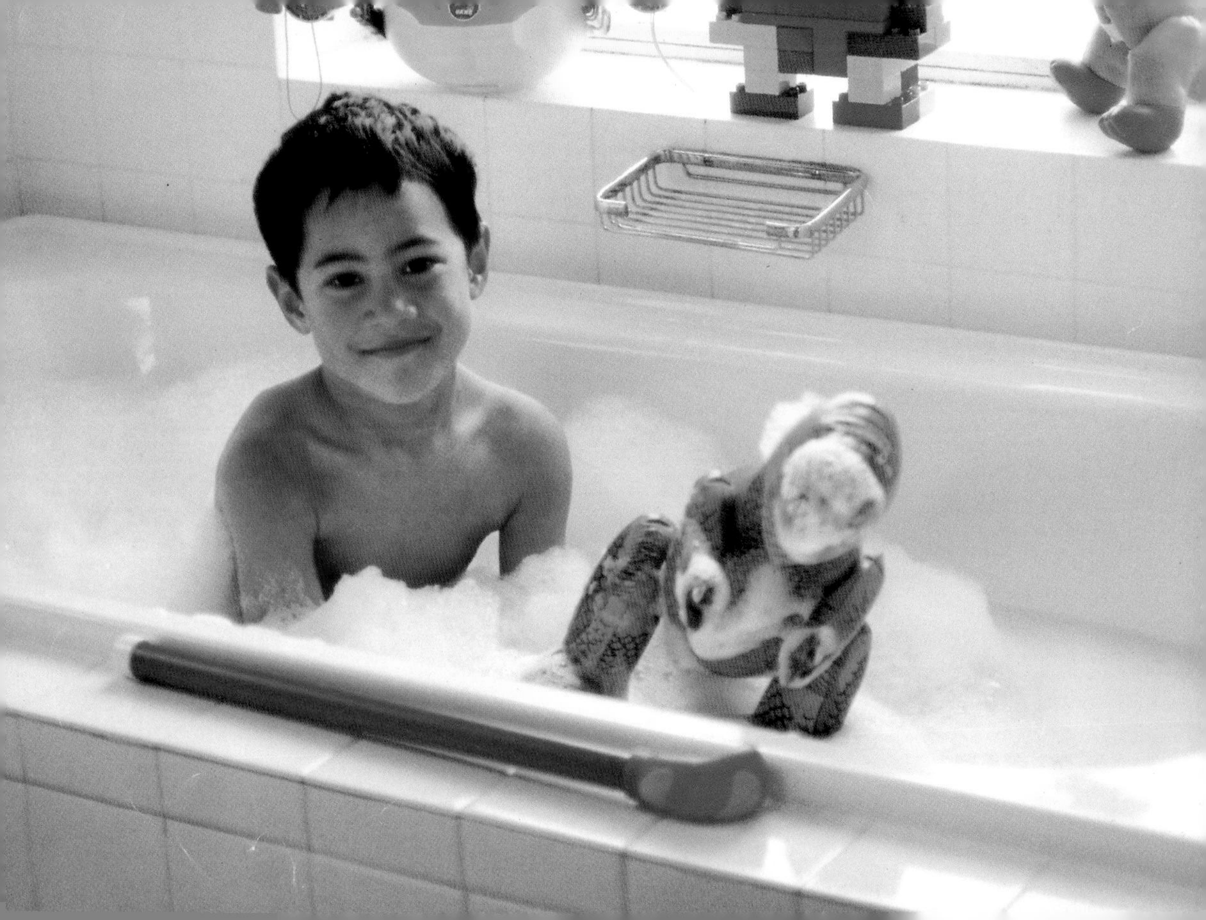

I am in bed.

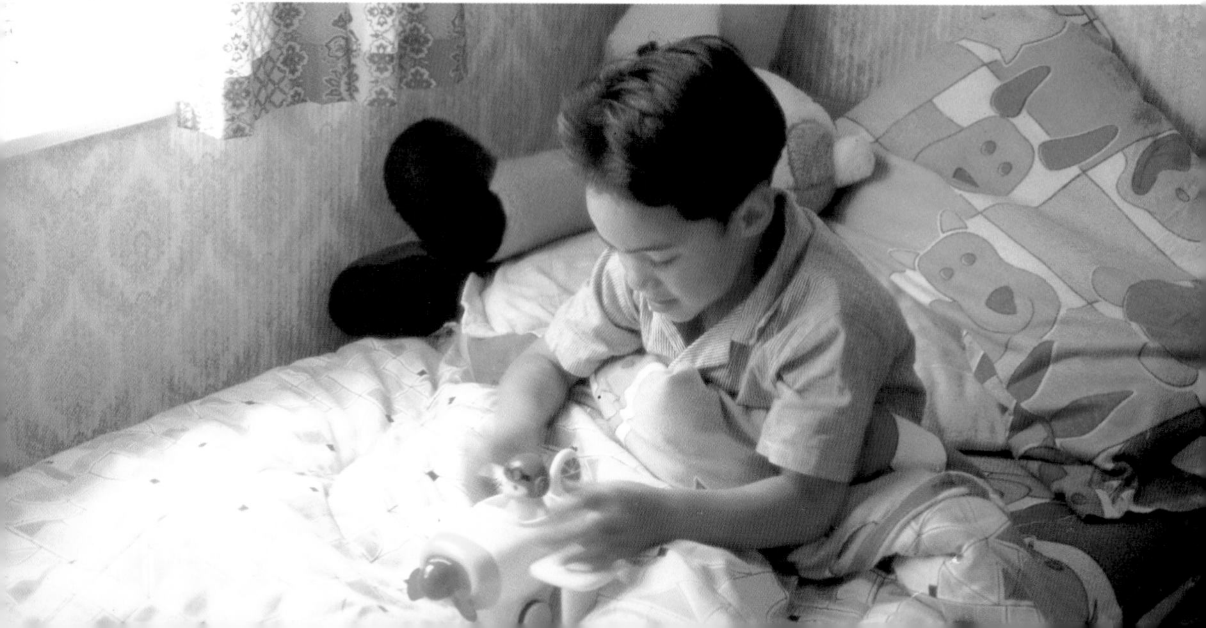